The Little Indian Weaver

BAH, THE LITTLE INDIAN WEAVER

The LITTLE INDIAN WEAVER

BY
MADELINE BRANDEIS

Producer of the Motion Pictures

"The Little Indian Weaver"
"The Wee Scotch Piper"
"The Little Dutch Tulip Girl"
"The Little Swiss Wood-Carver"

Distributed by Pathè Exchange, Inc., New York City

Photographic Illustrations by the Author

GROSSET & DUNLAP
PUBLISHERS   NEW YORK
by arrangement with the A. Flanagan Company

PRINTED IN THE UNITED STATES OF AMERICA

To every child of every land,
Little sister, little brother,
As in this book your lives unfold,
May you learn to love each other.

Note --- For her inspirational help on these stories, upon which my series of books and motion pictures, "Children of All Lands," is based, I wish to thank Mary Gibsone Whitlock, a dreamer of dreams, and a Mother in the true and glorious spirit of the word.

Madeline Brandeis

CONTENTS

BAH AND CORNELIA

The Little Indian Weaver

CHAPTER I

THE CORN EAR DOLL

How would you like to have a doll made from a corn ear? That is the only kind of doll that Bah ever thought of having. Bah was only five years old and she had never been away from her home, so of course she couldn't know very much.

But she knew a bit about weaving blankets, and she was learning more each day from her mother, who made beautiful ones and sold them.

You see, Bah and her mother were American Indians, and they belonged to the Navajo tribe. Their home was on the Navajo Reservation in Arizona, and they called it an Indian village. But if you went there you would not think it very much of a village in comparison to the villages you know.

As a matter of fact, all you could see was a row of funny little round houses, looking very much like large beehives, put together with mud and sticks and called hogans. A street of hogans in each of which lived a whole family of Indians, a few goats and sheep, a stray dog or two, an Indian woman sitting outside her hogan weaving a blanket, perhaps a child running with a dog—this, then, was a Navajo village.

THE LITTLE INDIAN WEAVER

How different from your villages with their smooth stone buildings, their stores and gasoline stations, and pretty shrub-covered bungalows!

Most Indian women have many babies, and the whole family lives to-

gether in one room which is the living room, bedroom, kitchen and dining
room all rolled into one. In the top
of the hogan is a hole, so that the
smoke from the cooking fire in the
middle of the room can go out.

Bah did not spend much time in her
hogan. No sooner was she up in the
morning than she was outside gather-
ing sticks for the breakfast fire. From
the time she put her little brown face
outside the hogan door, bright and
early in the morning, until nightfall
when she cuddled down in her warm
Navajo blanket, she was out in the
air—and the air is so fresh out there
in the desert; so much fresher than it
is in the big smoky cities.

Bah was a bright-eyed, healthy little girl, and the way she dressed will sound queer to you, for her clothes were made just like her mother's. On rainy days you have no doubt "dressed up" in mother's clothes and thought it quite a lark. But when the game was over, how glad you were to come back to your own little dresses and short socks.

But Bah had always dressed in the same way—and that is, in a long full cotton skirt, a calico waist with long sleeves, and many strings of bright beads about her neck. Her hair was long, black and shiny, and her mother tied it up in a knot at the back of her neck with a white cloth.

Every morning Bah had a lesson in weaving, just as you have a drawing lesson or a sewing lesson. Her father had made her a tiny loom which stood outside the hogan door next to her mother's big loom.

The morning when Bah planned the corn ear doll she was in the midst of her weaving lesson. Mother's fingers were flying in and out, and Bah's fingers were slow—oh, so slow, but her mind was not. Her mind was at work on a doll. She had once seen the picture of a doll, a real one. It was such a lovely doll! She wanted to cuddle it. How she would love to hug a doll close to her and rock it to sleep!

The corn was ripe in the field which was not far away. After the lesson she would pick an ear of corn, dry it nicely and dress it in a wee Indian blanket. She would make some beads for its neck. She would stick in two black beads for eyes. She would—

"Bah! you do not heed the lesson!"

It was Mother. And Mother was scolding. There were few times in Bah's life when she could remember Mother having been cross. Bah was at once attentive.

"I am sorry, Ma Shima (my mother)," she said, in the Navajo language. "I was dreaming of something sweet."

"It is bad medicine to dream when one is awake, Bah," said Mother.

"You will never learn to weave—and a Navajo woman who cannot weave blankets is indeed a useless one."

Bah hung her head in shame. But Mother laughed.

"Do not look that way, my little one, but try now to make the little pattern which I teach you."

Bah did try. She had to rip out several rows of bad weaving caused by her dreams of her corn ear doll. But not once, until the lesson was over, did Bah think again of the doll.

The weaving lesson was at last over, and Bah ran quickly to the cornfield, where she began to look eagerly for a proper ear of corn with which to make a proper Indian doll.

As she was looking through the many waving stalks, she thought she heard her name being called. But was it her name, and was it being called? It sounded more like singing than like calling—and Mother did not sing.

"Bah, Bah, Black Sheep
Have you any wool?"

This is what Bah heard.

She stopped in her search and looked around. There, a few yards away, was some one coming towards her on a pony. Bah's first thought was to run. She did not want to meet a stranger. So few came here to her home, where the only people the little girl ever saw were Mother, Father, and the few Indians who lived nearby.

White people were mysterious to Bah, and yet she often wondered about the white children and how they played and worked and what they did all day in school. Bah would go to school next year—to the big new school just built on the Reservation for Indian children. White people built it, and so it must be like the white children's school. Sometimes she longed to go—and other times she was just a little bit afraid.

"Yes, sir, yes, sir,
Three bags full."

The pony which Bah had seen from a distance was now standing beside her, and she could see the rider, al-

BAH'S HOME

though he could not see her, for she had hidden and was crouching between the cornstalks.

The rider was a very small person— a boy—a white boy. Bah really didn't feel as though he should be classified as white, for his skin was a mixture of orange and brown—orange where the sun had burned him, and over that a pattern of vivid brown freckles. Bah had never before seen anything like him, and it is no wonder that the timid little Indian hid herself.

The speckled boy took off his large cowboy hat and wiped his hot brow with a cowboy's handkerchief.

"Gee, it's hot, Peanuts," he said aloud to the pony. "And I'd like to know the way back—but looks as if we're lost."

Peanuts was presumably bored, for he let his head sink slowly, closed his eyes and patiently waited for the next move. None came.

Bah, in her hiding place, was as dumb, if not as bored, as Peanuts. She was tense with excitement, which obviously Peanuts was not, and did not take her eyes from the boy's face. His every move very much interested her. Here, then, was a white boy. He must be white, for he was not an Indian and he spoke English.

Bah understood English, and of that she was very proud. Her mother and father had always traded with the white man, so they had learned to speak English, and had wisely taught their little girl. Now how much easier it would be for Bah when she started to school.

But her knowledge did not help her

at the moment when she looked up from her cornstalk hiding place into the face of a live white boy. Indeed she had even decided to run away, and was crawling noiselessly through the corn.

"Baa, Baa, Black Sheep,"

again the boy began to sing as he started to turn away. Bah stopped crawling. He did sing her name. He wanted her to come back. Maybe she could help him find his way. And Oh! the pony was stepping all over the corn. Didn't he know better than to do that?

The cornstalks rustled. The pony jumped to the side, and the boy turned in his saddle and saw Bah standing.

"Oh, hello!" he said and turned back—the pony trampling upon a beautiful stalk of corn. "I didn't see you before. Where were you?"

Bah couldn't speak. She tried ever so hard, but the English words she knew so well would not come.

The boy jumped down from his pony and went up to her. There was a smile on his face and as he came closer she saw that his eyes were as blue as the sky. That part of him was pretty, thought Bah, even if his skin was not—and the smile was friendly. So she gained courage.

"You call my name?" she ventured.

The boy looked puzzled.

"No," he said, "I don't know your

name, but I'm glad I've found you."

Again he smiled, and this time Bah smiled too.

"My name Bah," she said, "and you say 'Bah, Bah, back skip'—I think you call me come back to you."

When it suddenly dawned upon the boy what she meant he opened his mouth very wide indeed and laughed so hard that Bah again began to be afraid. But he stopped suddenly, realizing perhaps that he had frightened her, and said:

"Oh, no. That is a song we sing about 'black sheep' that goes 'bah bah'! I didn't know you heard me singing it."

Bah looked a bit ashamed, and did

not offer a reply. The boy kept on talking—

"But, gee, where do you come from, Bah? Is your house around here?"

"Yes," said Bah. "Hogan over way. Bah come to find corn in cornfield."

"Oh, I see," said the boy, "for dinner, I guess."

"No," replied the Indian girl, looking up into his face, "Bah make so pretty doll from corn ear. Will dress in blanket and beads. You ever see little girl's doll?"

She looked so intent and innocent that the boy could not scoff at what would have been, among members of his own group at home, a subject entirely forbidden in the presence of

growing gentlemen. Dolls! What interest had he in dolls! But as he
looked into the upturned face of the
little brown maiden, he suddenly realized that she had never heard of a
boy's dislike for dolls; in fact, she had
probably never before met a white
boy nor seen a white doll.

"Oh, yes, plenty of 'em," answered
the white boy, "but never made of an
ear of corn—"

Then, seeing a shadow pass over her
face he resumed gallantly, "But it
ought to make a peach of a doll.
Maybe I could help you make it."

Now Bah was certain that she would
like the white boy. She had never
before had a human playmate, and

the feeling was a pleasant one. But she remembered that her new friend was lost.

"You no can find way home?" she asked.

The boy laughed.

"I guess you want to get rid of me," he said. Then, sobering, he resumed. "Yes, really, I'm lost. Peanuts and I have been wandering all morning. You see, we started from Tuba early and we just didn't watch the trails, so here we are."

"Oh, Tuba," said Bah, "not so very far. I show you how to go."

"But first I'll help you fix up a corn doll," said the boy. "We'll first have to find a good fat corn ear. Nice fat dolls are the best, don't you think so?"

As he talked he began looking through the cornstalks, and Bah watched him. He finally found what he considered to be an ideal ear, and together the two children made it into a doll, black bead eyes, cornsilk hair, blanket, and all.

"I have just the name for her," said the boy. "We'll call her 'Cornelia!' Shall we?"

Bah nodded happily. The name was a new one to her and she did not catch its meaning in relation to her beautiful new doll, but it pleased her nevertheless. In fact, everything about the boy pleased her, and she was sorry when at last he said:

BAH AND CORNELIA

"It must be getting late. You'd better tell me how to get home. Mother will wonder what happened."

Bah pointed out directions and the boy, thanking her, held out his hand and said: "You never even asked my name. Don't you want to know?"

Bah drooped her head shyly as she replied: "Indian never ask name. Very bad manner."

The white boy's eyes opened wide.

"That's funny," he said. "Then how do you get to know people's names?"

"When one people like other people, they tell name. No ask," said Bah seriously.

"Oh, then I'll tell you quick 'cause I like you. My name's Billy."

Bah did not reply, but stood watching Billy as he swung himself onto his pony. Then, when he was seated and smiled down at her, she smiled up sweetly and said:

"We have cow named Billy."

BILLY

CHAPTER II

For days Bah's chief delight was her new corn ear doll. She kept it with her constantly. It went to bed with her, sat at meals with her, and watched the daily weaving lesson.

But one day a terrible thing happened. She was sitting by her mother's side outside the hogan, her little fingers flying through the strings of her loom, and one eye watching Mother's more experienced fingers as they made a beautiful new pattern.

Cornelia had been carefully dressed in her blanket, her beads hung about

32

THE WEAVING LESSON

her neck and fondly kissed by her de-
voted parent, and was now lying at
Bah's feet while the little girl worked
hard at her lesson.

"Pull your wool tighter, Bah," said
Mother, in Navajo.

Bah's fingers and tongue worked together. Children's tongues have a habit of moving with whatever else is in motion.

And as Bah worked, some sheep came wandering in from the field. They were tame sheep and often nosed about the hogan for a bit of human company or food, as the case might be, and this morning I fear the reason was food.

Father sheep was very large and therefore hungrier than the rest. His hunger made him bold. But Bah was a particular friend of his, and I doubt whether even his appetite could have driven him to do what he did that morning, had he been able to guess the great sorrow he was to cause.

"You have left out a stitch, my child, and there will be a hole in the work."

Bah's fingers stopped and so did her tongue.

"Oh dear, must I do that all over again, Mother?" she asked.

"If you wish to weave perfectly so that you may some day sell your work, then you must learn to rip and go over many times."

Ripping is deadly work, as everyone who has ever ripped knows. And Bah was not as interested in ripping as she had been in making her pattern. So her thoughts naturally turned to her precious Cornelia lying at her feet.

Her eyes turned at the same time,

and horror upon horrors, what did she see? The big black sheep was there chewing contentedly, but Cornelia was gone. The little blanket was there—so were the beads and some of the cornsilk hair. But Cornelia was gone. The sheep went on chewing and couldn't understand why Bah did not caress him as usual.

"Bah, do pay attention to your work!"

Mother was annoyed. Bah turned around and Mother saw a very sad sight. She saw before her another mother—a stricken little mother whose child had just provided a meal for a hungry animal. She rocked an empty blanket back and forth, and the

"GO AWAY, MR. SHEEP!"

tears were beginning to gather. Mother understood what had happened, and now her voice sounded soft and kind.

"Poor Bah! Your doll is gone!"

The little girl was crying as she continued to hug the empty blanket.

"Do not cry, my little one," said Mother. "Are there not many more corn ears in the field?"

"Yes, my Mother," sobbed the child, "but no more Cornelias!"

And that was final. Never again could Bah go back to the cornfield. Never again! How could Mother even have suggested such a thing! Didn't she know that Cornelia, since the day of her birth, had been different from all other ears of corn?

Why, Cornelia was a doll—she and Billy had decided that—and the rest were vegetables! Oh, didn't Mother understand? Perhaps Mother did, for her next remark showed it.

"One day, Bah, when I went to the

Trading Post near Tuba I saw a most beautiful doll. She was an Indian baby—a papoose—and she was strapped upon the prettiest little laced baby cradle you ever saw. She was dressed in a bright blanket and she had real hair and such lovely beads around her neck."

A smile was trying to chase away the tears on the face of the little mother as she listened to her own mother's recital of something too wonderful to imagine. She said sorrowfully: "Some white child will buy her, and how happy she will be. Ah, how I should like to have her."

Mother said: "And so you shall, if you will work to have her."

Bah's eyes asked the question: "How?" and her mother went on: "You know, Bah, that Mother sells or trades blankets, and that Father sells or trades his beautiful silver and matrix jewelry to the Trading Post. We do this so that we may have, in return, things which we want and need. Now, you want and need a little doll. Why not sell your work? Bah must weave a little blanket and take it to the store where they will perhaps trade with you for the papoose doll."

"Do you really think they will, Ma Shima?" asked Bah as if she could hardly believe it, and she wiped away her tears.

HOW BAH LONGED FOR THE PAPOOSE DOLL!

"Yes, I do," answered Mother. "But your blanket must be well made and of a pretty pattern—else they will not take it, for they, in turn, must sell it to the tourists."

"Then I shall make the most beautiful blanket which has ever been made," laughed Bah, now thoroughly interested in her new task with its wonderful object.

She worked all through the morning on her little blanket, with happy thoughts of a real-haired Indian doll flying through her mind as her fingers flew through her work. It was not until she heard Mother grinding the corn for lunch that she looked up, and not until then that she thought again of the morning's sorrow. But then she did think of it, and her parents wondered why she could not eat her corn bread.

CHAPTER III

AT THE TRADING POST

Billy's mother and father had come to Arizona for a special reason. Billy's father was a writer, and he had come for information on the Navajo Indians for a new book he was writing. Every day he would go to the Indian villages, sit among the big chiefs and medicine men (who are the wise ones among the Indians and are supposed to work charms which cure the sick) and he would jot down in his notebook many things which they told him.

Billy went with his father the first

few days, but he didn't care much for
the way they sat around and did nothing but talk. Billy was a very active
boy and he soon grew tired of listen-
ing to the droning voices of the Indian men, and the scratching of Father's pencil. At last he told Father
how it was, and Father laughed.

"I thought you were going to write,
too, Billy," he said. "You'll never find
out about the Indians if you don't take
the trouble to listen—and then you'll
never win that composition contest
you've been dreaming about."

It was true that Billy, since he had
left New York, had dreamed of nothing else but the composition contest.
Many of his friends at home were al-

Navajo Indian Trading Post.

"I TRADE MY BLANKET FOR PAPOOSE DOLL!"

ready struggling with their composi-
tions, for the prize was worth striving
for—a wonderful radio set, the very
latest model.

And how the others had envied him,
for he was to go to Arizona and live

among the Indians where he would be
sure to learn so much of interest and
send in a true account of the lives of
American Indians. The contest was
open to any composition dealing with
children of any particular race or
country, and was to reveal their
habits and customs.

"Oh! You'll win it easily, Bill," his
chum had said. "Indians are such interesting people, and you'll find out all
about them if you stick to your dad."

And Billy had been fired with ambi-
tion, when he had left, and when
he had first arrived. But the novelty
of the idea was gradually wearing
off and he seemed to like far more
to gallop over the country on

his pony, Peanuts, than to glean knowledge. Especially since his meeting with Bah did he look forward each morning to his ride. And each day he tried to find the Indian girl and went many times to the cornfield. But she was never there and, try as he might, Billy could not find her village.

Father did not wait for Billy to answer him, but said: "Well, old man, I can see the radio set gradually taking wings and broadcasting itself! You'll never win it this way, you know—and you'd have a good chance, too, if you'd come along and listen to some of the old fellows I'm chumming with each day."

"Oh, I'll come along tomorrow, Dad,"

said Billy carelessly. "Today I'm going to the Trading Post and see the Indian stuff there."

"Well, do as you like, Son," said his father, "but don't be annoyed if you don't win the contest."

"I'll write something yet, Dad, you'll see."

Peanuts and Billy found themselves at the Trading Post in the heat of the day. Billy tied the pony in the shade and went into the store. It was filled with a mixed assortment of objects. On one side of the room were groceries, pots and pans, cigarettes, in fact a little bit of everything necessary for housekeeping. On the other side were the Indian curios—silver and matrix jewelry, beautifully fashioned with blue stones set in, handsome Navajo blankets hanging on the wall, pottery of all kinds, and beads, beads, beads.

Billy wandered about the store and he thought of his mother, and how she would like something to take home as a souvenir. The beads looked hopeful, as he could carry them, while a pottery jar or blanket would be big and heavy. Taking from his pocket his two dollars and some few cents, he selected the string of beads which looked most likely.

One string in particular very much pleased him. It was delicately made, but looked simple enough to be within

reach of his two dollars. The shop-
keeper was chewing tobacco in the
corner. He was a white man made
brown by the Arizona sun and wind.

"How much is this string?" asked
Billy, holding it up for the man to see.

"That one's fifty dollars!"

"Fifty what?" asked Billy, dazed.

"Fifty dollars, Son," repeated the
man, "and that's one of the cheapest."

"Gee whiz," sighed Billy. "I'm out
with my two an' a quarter!"

"Yes," smiled the man. "No one
knows how much work the Injuns put
into that stuff. It's all handmade, and
their tools ain't so good either, so it
takes 'em a long time. But they sure
know how to make 'em."

"You bet they do," said Billy—and just then his eye fell on a doll, a papoose it was, with a blanket and a string of beads. He thought of Cornelia and smiled to himself. How Bah would open her eyes if she could see this one!

As he was thinking about her, he suddenly decided to try once more to find her. Maybe this storekeeper knew where the village was. He asked—the storekeeper knew of several not far away.

"The Indians come in every day with things to trade. It's funny how they like plain stuff like beans and salt and will trade beautiful jewelry and bankets for just plain sacks of food.

But we try and treat 'em fair. It would be easy though to cheat 'em. They don't know how valuable their stuff is."

"But you don't!" said Billy.

"No, we don't. Indians are honest, and white men should treat 'em honestly!"

"That's right," said Billy, thinking of the only Indian he ever knew, and deciding to be off in search of her home.

As he stepped out of the door he saw a small figure trudging along towards the Trading Post with what looked like a small blanket thrown over her arm. As she came closer he recognized Bah and ran to meet her.

"Gee, I'm glad to see you, Bah," he cried. "Do you know I've been looking for you ever since the day we made Cornelia. Do you remember?"

Bah was smiling happily, but upon mention of that name her face fell.

"Why, what's the matter, Bah? Wasn't she a good doll?"

"Cornelia ate up!" said Bah, slowly.

"Ate up what?" asked Billy.

"Sheep—big one—"

"Gee, what an appetite she must have had!" laughed Billy. But seeing that his friend was taking the conversation seriously he stopped laughing and asked: "What do you mean?"

"Big sheep come—very hungry. Eat up Cornelia!"

"Aw, that is too bad!" said Billy.

But now it was Bah's turn to smile. She held out her blanket and said: "You see Bah's blanket. Bah come to trade blanket for doll in Trading Post. So pretty doll, Ma Shima said!"

Billy remembered the papoose doll and was delighted to think that it would really belong to his friend.

"That's great," he said. "May I go along with you while you trade? I never saw anyone trade and I'd like to watch you."

"Me never trade before," said the Indian girl softly, and it seemed to Billy that her voice trembled.

"Poor little kid," he said to himself. "She's scared stiff!"

He went into the store with Bah and watched her as she walked up to the man in the corner and handed him the blanket. Then she pointed to the doll—but she said nothing. The man took the blanket and examined it. He knew immediately what she wanted.

He understood Indians. And as he looked at the blanket a smile passed over his face, and Billy noticed for the first time that the blanket was far from perfect.

There was a hole in it, and some of the threads were sticking out. Oh, it was not a very well made blanket when one compared it with the works of art hanging on the wall.

As the man smiled to himself Billy's

anger rose. Wasn't she only a little
girl? How could they expect her to
weave as well as the women did? It
was wonderful that she could do that
well! Why, he didn't know a girl at
home who could even start to weave
a blanket like that. He felt his fists
clenching together as he watched the
man's face. At last the man spoke.
He spoke only two words as he handed
Bah her blanket.

"No trade."

The Indian girl looked at him for a
moment, and Billy saw two small lakes
in her eyes. She did not wait for them
to overflow, but ran out of the store,
holding her little blanket tight.

Billy came to himself after she had

"PRETTY PAPOOSE DOLL."

flown through the door, and made a start as though to follow her. But he stopped and turned.

"How much is that doll, mister?" he asked abruptly.

"That doll's two an' a half, Son."

"Well, I'll give you two twenty-five for her, an' that's all," said a voice that Billy could hardly believe was his own, so big and manly did it sound.

The man looked at him for a moment and then evidently seeing something he liked in the boy's eyes, said:

"All right, sonny. It's yours. And you can bet that Indian kid will never forget you!"

Without another word the boy paid his money, took the doll which the man wrapped for him, and departed.

Outside the Post, when Billy mounted his pony, his thought was, naturally, to go to Bah and deliver the doll. The distress which he had seen in the eyes of his little friend made him realize just what a disappointment she had had.

But, alas, Billy knew no more of Bah's whereabouts than he had known before seeing her at the Trading Post. The man had said that there were three or four small Indian villages nearby, but the question was in which one did Bah live? He jumped down again from his pony and ran into the store: "Say, Mister, do you know where that little girl lives?" he asked.

"No," came the answer. "I never saw her before. The old folks seldom bring their kids when they come to trade. Anyway not into the Post. They leave 'em outside most times to watch the burro."

So a period of searching began for Billy. That day he visited one of the villages. He looked at each hogan for Bah, and asked the Indians he met, but she did not live there. They all shook their heads and grunted when he asked:

"Bah, little girl, live here?"

It was very discouraging because he couldn't tell whether they had even understood him. It grew late and he had to hurry home for fear of worrying his parents.

The next day he started out early, determined to try the other villages, and he left a puzzled father, who remarked to his wife as the boy disappeared on a fast gallop:

BILLY RIDING THROUGH THE INDIAN VILLAGE

"Bill isn't taking the interest in the Indians I had hoped he would."

But Mother smiled wisely.

"He's getting brown and strong, though," she answered, "and that's better."

CHAPTER IV

THE PRAYER STICK

Bah was making a prayer stick. The prayer stick is an old custom among the Indians, and every Indian child knows about it. But Bah had never wanted anything badly enough to try the charm. Now, it was the only thing left for her to do.

She took the branch of a tree, a straight branch which she cleaned, and then she took the feather of an eagle. She tied the feather to the end of the stick with a bit of wool from her loom. She wrapped the wool around and around, and when the feather was se-

THE PRAYER STICK

cure in place she made a hole in the
ground and put the other end of the
stick into the hole. The stick stood
up straight and the feather on top of
it waved slightly in the breeze.

Bah stood over her handiwork,

raised her two arms skyward and prayed: "Oh, Prayer Stick," she chanted in Navajo, "please take my prayer to the sky on this eagle's feather! My prayer is for a doll!"

Now, you may think that Bah was idol-worshipping—that she didn't know better than to pray to a stick and a feather! But this was not the case. She knew very well that it was the Great Father who saw and heard all, but her ancestors had all used the eagle feather to convey to the Great Father their prayers and to tell Him their needs.

It was only a method of reaching her God. When her people wanted the rain to fall they danced the great

Eagle Dance for rain, and the Great Father saw and understood. This prayer of Bah's was only her way of asking what you would no doubt ask with your eyes closed and your hands folded together.

She did not know that she was being watched. As she started her prayer, Billy had approached the hogan. His first thought had been to call to her, but somehow he had felt that what she was doing was not to be interrupted, so he stopped.

It was not his intention to listen secretly to something he had no right to hear. But as he stopped, she prayed so loudly that he could not help hearing and, anyway, she did not seem to care for she went on and on, regardless of the fact that she was out in broad daylight, in front of her hogan, and anyone might pass before her door.

The prayer was repeated, and it was not until she had recited it many times that she lowered her arms and with them her gaze from the heavens, and beheld the white boy standing a few yards away. He stood holding his pony's bridle with one hand, and the other hand was behind his back. He looked at her questioningly and then at the Prayer Stick, whose feather was waving back and forth. Bah smiled and said: "I make this prayer stick to pray for doll."

"THEN BAH GIVE IT TO YOU."

It was hard for the boy to grasp her meaning, for he knew so little about the Indians and their queer customs. However, he smiled back at her and, keeping his hand behind him, asked: "Where is the blanket you made, Bah?"

"You like to see?" she questioned sweetly.

"Yes, please," said Billy.

Bah went towards the hogan and took from a nail the blanket she had failed to sell. It was hanging on the outside wall of the hogan, a proof that it was appreciated here if not at the Trading Post. Bah brought it over and held it up for Billy to see.

"You like?" she asked innocently, cocking her head on one side like a little sparrow.

"I like very much, Bah," answered Billy eagerly. "I like to—"

Bah did not allow him to finish his sentence, but, starting to drape the blanket about his shoulders, she smilingly said: "Then Bah give to you!"

The boy stood amazed while the little Indian girl patted the blanket into place on his shoulders. She was giving him the blanket which she had tried so hard to trade. It was really spoiling everything for him. He had hoped to make quite a dramatic scene out of the trade, and the doll was to be a genuine surprise. Now it looked as though Bah had forgotten the doll and even the blanket, for she gave it up so easily and was standing in front of him smiling sweetly.

"I'll trade you something for the blanket, Bah," he began.

"Oh, no—Bah give—no trade!"

It was settled. Billy could see that

by the look in her eyes. He brought forth his package.

"Then Billy will give Bah this," he exclaimed, holding out the bundle to her. Solemnly Bah looked into his face. Her eyes seemed to ask many questions but she said nothing. Billy understood. He tore the string, undid the package, and the girl's eyes never left his face. It was as though she had guessed what was there. She looked down and beheld in his hands— the doll!

Her mouth opened and she formed only the word "Oh"—Billy put the papoose doll into her arms. Slowly and solemnly she kissed it. Then, turning quickly she ran to her mother who

"AND BILLY GIVE BAH THIS."

was weaving in the accustomed
place—

"Ma Shima, oh, Ma Shima! The papoose doll! She is mine. The Great
Father has sent her!"

It was all in Navajo and Billy did not

understand. He watched her as she sat down beside her mother and held up her new treasure. He heard her mother emit sounds, though he could hardly see her lips moving. Had he been able to understand Navajo he would have heard some very sweet and happy words.

Then Bah's mother looked over at Billy. She beckoned him to come and he came. Her black, beady eyes followed him until he stood before her. He did not know what to think of the smile she gave him. Was it friendly, or was she mocking him?

Billy had never before met an Indian woman, and he was puzzled by the black eyes so deep and mysterious.

BAH AND THE PAPOOSE DOLL

Billy found himself staring, and was suddenly aware of himself standing before a lady with his hat on. He doffed his sombrero and in doing so he smiled. Bah's mother smiled back, and said in a musical voice, "Sit down."

"WHITE BOY GOOD FRIEND TO INDIAN!"

He sat beside her. Bah was on her other side, absorbed in her doll. Billy smiled into the face of the Indian woman and she put her arm about him and said:

"White boy good friend to Indian!"

CHAPTER V

AT BAH'S HOGAN

"Why do you call her 'Bah?' Is it because she watches the sheep?"

Billy was asking many questions of Bah's mother and he found her anxious and ready to answer him. She had already told him her name, which showed that she liked him, and Billy was pleased. He wanted to hear many things about this family, especially about his little friend, Bah.

Her mother shook her head. "No, not why. I tell you story why we call her Bah." And this is what Bah's Mother told Billy:

Many Indians name their babies in this way: Soon after the baby is born, the mother straps it to the baby cradle and goes to the door of her hogan—what she first sees as she looks out upon the world, is what she calls her newborn. If she sees a running deer—then the baby is called "Running Deer." If her first glance falls upon a lazy bull, resting himself, the baby will bear the name of "Sitting Bull."

Then, there is another way of naming the Indian baby, and this is the way Bah was named. When she was a wee papoose, her mother would make the bread and set her down beside the stone oven where she could

WHEN BAH WAS A PAPOOSE

watch from her baby cradle. As you
perhaps know, the Indian baby cradle
is very plain, and simply made.
It is only a board upon which the baby
is strapped until he is able to walk. The
Indians have some very good reasons

for doing this. They wish to train children to be uncomfortable and not to cry.

Strapped as they are to this board, they are only able to move their hands and must lie straight and stiff. This is also the reason why all Indians are so straight. Then the Indian mother's mind is at rest, when she can have her baby securely tied in the cradle, strapped to her back, or if she puts him down any place she knows that he is safe. She can hang him on the wall while she works, which was what Bah's mother did when she made the bread.

Now, bread in Navajo is "Bah," and this is how they make it. First, they take some corn and put it into a hollow stone. With another stone they smash the corn until it is fine. They then mix it with water, knead it and flatten it into small flat cakes which look like pancakes. It then goes into the big stone oven, which is always out of doors, and when it is cooked it is taken out and placed on a cool stone.

At this point Bah, who you see was at that time only a papoose, would cry and reach out her little hands for some "Bah". As soon as Mother would put a crisp piece into her little hand she would stop crying and chew on it contentedly. So they called her "Bah" because she cried for bread.

"So your name is 'Bread!' That's a

BAH GETS HER NAME

nice name. And I'm so hungry that I could eat you now!" said Billy, rising to his feet and making a pretense at biting.

Bah laughed and hid her face behind the new doll. Mother chuckled to herself, as Indians do when they are amused. Then she said: "I make some real 'Bah' for you."

"Oh, that would be fine!" said the boy.

Then, realizing that he had practically asked for it, he hung his head and added: "But don't do it if it's too much trouble."

The remark seemed to amuse the Indian woman, for she chuckled again as she arose, but she did not answer him. Instead, she began to prepare for the making of the bread.

Billy watched the process with great interest, and ate with even more interest when it was finished. The Bah was delicious, he thought.

It tasted like—no, it didn't taste like

anything Billy had ever eaten before.

After having done justice to the new food, the boy was shown in and about the hogan by his little friend. She took him to her "play hogan." It was made for her by her father and was just like the one they lived in, except that it was only large enough for one child to fit into.

"We could have lots of fun here, Bah. I'd like to come again and play with you. May I?" Billy asked.

"Yes, come much," answered Bah happily.

"And we'll play that I'm an Indian Chief and you are the Indian Mother, and the doll—oh, we haven't named the doll yet, have we?" said Billy.

"No, doll no name yet," said Bah.

"Well, let's see, how shall we do it?" Billy mused. "Suppose you come out of your play hogan and look around. The first thing you see will be what we'll name her."

"Yes, I do," said Bah—and obediently she entered the small hogan.

"Now come out, but close your eyes," called Billy.

Out came the little girl, holding her papoose doll. She stood, with closed eyes, in the door of her hogan, and waited for further instructions.

"Open your eyes!" called the boy, "and tell me what you see!"

Bah's eyes opened slowly, dramatically. Her head was raised and as she

NAMING THE PAPOOSE DOLL

looked she saw a bluebird in a tree. Billy followed her gaze and saw what she did.

"How lucky!" thought he, "Now the child will have a beautiful name!"

But Bah looked down at her baby

and smilingly said: "Bah name you 'Doli'."

Billy was horribly disappointed. "Oh, listen, Bah. Don't do that! Why every girl calls a doll 'dol-ly.' That's common—name her 'Blue-bird.' You saw one, didn't you?"

Bah was still smiling as she said: "Yes, I see and I name papoose 'Blue-bird' in Navajo—that is 'Doli'."

A grin spread from one of Billy's ears to the other. "That's the time you fooled me!" said he.

They were laughing over Bah's joke when they saw some one coming to-wards them. "My father come home," cried Bah, and ran to meet him.

As he came nearer Billy saw that he

was very tall and very straight. He wore white trousers tied below the knees with red ribbons, a sash about his waist, and many beads hanging from his neck. His hair was long and tied in the back, much the same as Bah's, with a white cloth.

He came over and held out his hand to Billy. He said: "I hear you good to little Bah. Me Bah's father."

Billy was thrilled to shake the hand of such a fine big Indian, and to find that he was treating him as a friend.

"He Big Chief," said Bah proudly.

"Oh, are you a Big Chief?" asked the boy. A thought began to flicker through his mind. He would surprise his father—his father who was hob-

nobbing daily with Big Chiefs and
Medicine Men, and who thought Billy
was wasting his time.

He wouldn't say a word to Father,
but he'd begin tonight and he'd write
a story, all about Bah, her mother and
her father, the Big Chief. He'd come
back again tomorrow and learn more
from them, for hadn't Bah said "Come
much"—which meant he was welcome.

"Well, I have had such a good time
with Bah—Mr. -a -a"

"My name 'Fighting Bull,' " said the
brave (as Indian men are called).

"I know why you're called Fighting
Bull," said Billy, sagely. "One time
when you were little your Mother
must have seen a bull fight!"

CHAPTER VI

BILLY STARTS HIS STORY

The next morning found Billy fully dressed and ready to leave before his parents were even awake. He could hardly wait for them to be astir and as soon as he heard his mother's step in her room he knocked at the door. Mother opened it and stood amazed.

"Why, Billy—at this hour! What do you mean?"

"I'm going out, Mother, and I didn't want to leave before you were awake."

"But, dear, you can't go so early, and without your breakfast."

"Oh, that's all right. Peanuts and I

will go to the Trading Post and get breakfast. You see, Mother, I have to—"

Just then there came a growl from within the room. It came from Father.

"What is the commotion? And at such an hour! Billy, what's the excitement?"

"Nothing, Father—only it's such a fine morning and I want a ride."

"Let him go, Mother. He is only keeping me from my hard-earned rest. When one works one needs sleep. Billy will never need it!"

Billy was sharp enough to understand his father's words and, smiling shrewdly to himself, he clutched a paper which reposed in his pocket, but he only called out, "Goodby, Father."

His mother kissed him with the parting words: "Do be careful, Billy, and don't go too far."

"No further than usual, Mother," answered Billy.

And then, afraid that Mother might ask something, he ran off, waving his hand and sighing a deep sigh of relief.

Billy had spent some restless hours during the night, thinking about the story he was to write. As he was only a little boy and couldn't write very well, and as this was his very first story, he was a little bit afraid of the results.

But the determination to surprise Father and Mother had grown within

BAH'S MOTHER WEAVING NAVAJO BLANKET

him ever since the idea had come to him yesterday at Bah's home. Father thought Billy couldn't do it! Well, he'd show him! He'd listen while Mrs. Fighting Bull told him things, and hadn't he already learned lots about them?

In fact, he'd started his story! He'd started it with a poem (at least he thought it a poem) and that is what he clutched in his pocket when Father chided him. He was going to show it to Bah and her mother.

He was going to ask them what they thought of it and he was going to tell them all about the contest, and how he'd planned to win the radio without telling his parents!

How astonished they'd be, and how Father would stare when he saw the radio arrive with his son's name engraved thereon—

"Winner of Composition Contest."

His dreams accompanied Billy all the way to the Trading Post. There he

BAH'S FATHER STRETCHING A SKIN

had a hurried breakfast of milk and crackers, allowed Peanuts to graze a bit in the clover, and after buying some funny chocolates in the forms of objects, animals, birds and fishes which he thought would amuse Bah, he was

off in search of his new-made friends
—and information.

Upon arriving at the hogan he found
Bah's mother already seated at her
loom. Fighting Bull was stretching a
goat's skin outside the hogan door.

After greeting the Indians, Billy
looked around for Bah. She was no-
where to be seen.

"Where's Bah?" he asked of her
mother. The woman shook her head,
the usual amused smile playing over
her features. "Not here."

The Indians had not seemed particularly pleased to see him, he thought,
and his heart was beginning to sink.
But then Bah's mother pointed towards the play hogan. "Over there.

She play mother and papoose.   See?"

With these words, Mrs. Fighting Bull laughed out loud, a sort of chuckle it was, but nevertheless she did laugh, and Billy felt reassured. He looked and saw Bah.

She was emerging from her play hogan, and there was something on her back. He couldn't tell what it was, but as she approached he saw that it was a large board with a blanket strapped around it. Something was in the blanket, and that something was heavy, too, for Bah was obviously weighted down.

"What's that?" asked Billy, puzzled.

"That my papoose," laughed Bah, and turning her back towards Billy he

BAH'S PAPOOSE

saw, strapped cozily to the papoose
cradle, a baby sheep! It was bleating,
"Baa, Baa–"

"He knows your name," laughed Billy, stroking the small woolly head.

Bah sat down with her burden on her

back and Billy sat beside her. The Indian mother continued to smile to herself as she went on weaving.

"Me glad you come," said Bah, smiling her friendly smile.

"Are you?" questioned Billy. "I couldn't wait to get here. You know, I've started to write a story—a real story like Father writes. It's going to be all about you!"

"Me?" the little girl pointed to herself. She realized that this was something important, for the white boy was excited and although the affair was very vague to her, she mustered up the enthusiasm necessary.

"I've written a poem to start it with. Want to hear it?"

"Oh, yes," Bah's eyes grew big. Just what a poem was didn't matter. It was important to know that Billy had written one. So he read—

> "Bah, Bah Indian girl,
> Have you any bread?
> Yes sir, yes sir,
> That's what I was fed.
> When I was a papoose
> I cried to my ma,
> So she gave me bread,
> And now my name is 'Bah'!"

There was a loud explosion from the corner where Mrs. Fighting Bull was weaving. Billy's face grew red. Mrs. Fighting Bull was laughing at him. Oh, now he knew he must have done something wrong!

The Indian woman composed herself and beckoning the boy over, she said:

"You write good words. Tell me more."

Billy had a great deal to learn about Indians; he was beginning to realize that. Evidently Bah's mother was kindly disposed towards him but she had a queer way of laughing at everything, which was hard for Billy to understand.

Still, he thought, it was better to laugh at everything than to be cross and angry. Mrs. Fighting Bull was a jolly woman, that was all, and Billy moved up close to her and smiled up into her face.

"Gee, I'm glad you like it. I thought, when you laughed, you were making fun of me. You see, I never wrote anything before, and this story has just got to be good, because— --"

And then he told Bah and her mother of his desire to win the contest and the prize attached to it.

"You like I tell you more?" asked the Indian woman.

"That's just what I'd like to have you do, if you would," answered the boy writer.

"Well, I tell you."

With no more ado, Mrs. Fighting Bull started talking as Billy sat and listened to her words.

CHAPTER VII

ALL ABOUT THE INDIANS

The Navajo Indians live in hogans. That, you already have heard — and you know what a hogan looks like. But all Indian tribes do not use the same kind of dwelling places.

The Pueblo, Hopi and other peaceful tribes live in what are called pueblos. They are houses built of adobe and they are built to resemble a child's stone blocks when he has piled one on top of the other. To reach the top of a pueblo one must climb the ladders which are set up against the outside of the building.

The Pueblo villages are different from the Navajo villages. They are composed of long rows of these pinkish adobe block houses, and the Indian tribes who live therein are, as I have said, peaceful.

Can you imagine why, being as they are of a peaceful nature, these tribes build as they do? It is so that they can be protected from warlike tribes, in their many storied houses. Then, too, the tribes which build pueblos do not wander, as the warlike tribes do. The pueblos are stationary, and they are built to be permanent homes. They are built, mainly, by the women and children, who do all the manual work— while the men often sit at home weav-

THE PIPE OF PEACE

ing garments and knitting stockings.
The tepees are the abode of warlike
Indians, such as the Sioux, Apaches, etc.
They wander and so they build tem-
porary dwellings which, at a moment's
notice, may be transported quickly and

easily from one location to another.

In the East there are other Indian tribes, and also in Canada. Then, in Mexico, the Indians build straw huts.

There are hundreds of tribes of Indians and each tribe has a different language. That is why the sign language came into existence. It is used when a member of one tribe meets a member of another tribe. They cannot understand each other's language, so they talk with their hands.

When the Indian chiefs gather they smoke the pipe of peace. This is usually done to celebrate some victory, or upon the occasion of a visit from a member of another tribe.

The men sit around a fire in a circle

THE FIRE MAKER

and pass the long pipe from one to the other. As each man receives it he utters a sound or nods his head, proceeds to take a puff, and passes it to his neighbor. It is all done silently and quietly, but there is a wealth of meaning in this very solemn performance.

The Indians, in older days, made fire entirely by friction. By the rubbing together of two pieces of wood, most of the tribes caused fire to appear— but some had elaborate devices made of wood and string. The Navajos used a thin pole which they twirled around by using a string tied to a stick.

Today, the Indians use matches just as we do, but most families still keep their fire-makers.

The Navajos do not use feathers and do not make chiefs by crowning them. But many of the other tribes create their chiefs by placing the crown of tall feathers, which you have often seen in pictures, upon the head of the

CROWNING A BIG CHIEF

"brave," and saying "I make you 'Big Chief Flying Eagle,'" or whatever the name may be.

The eagle is much venerated by the Indians. We have seen how Bah used a prayer stick made of an eagle feather.

In the Eagle Dance, the dancer paints his body red, black and white, and wears a dance skirt and bonnet of eagle feathers.

The dance is performed as a ceremonial, mostly as a plea for rain. The dancers imitate almost every movement of the great eagle. They soar, they hover as an eagle would hover over the fields. They spread their wings and move about in a great circle.

This and the Sun Dance are the two most important and interesting dances of the Indians; the Sun Dance is performed in the spring, celebrating the return of the growing season, and the growth of the corn.

"Oh, I hope I can remember all that,"

sighed Billy, when Mrs. Fighting Bull finished talking.

She turned to her weaving without answering him, and he turned to Bah, saying: "Come, Bah! Let us play over at your hogan and you pretend to make me a Big Chief!"

"Yes, come," said Bah, rising.

They started over to their play house. From out the play hogan Bah pulled forth some Navajo blankets and then they both set to work to make a feather crown. Having no feathers (the Navajos not using them) they made their crown of branches.

It was a large and weighty object when they finished with it and Billy was, indeed, a queer sight when Bah placed it upon his head. The big blanket was wrapped about him, and from beneath the crown peered his freckled face. With all due ceremony Bah raised her eyes to heaven and chanted: "I make you Big Chief Spots-In-The-Face!"

It was a very serious moment for them. Billy had become a chief, and his next move was to propose the smoking of the pipe of peace. From his pocket Billy pulled a chocolate pipe. It was done up in silver paper. Bah was impressed as he carefully unwrapped and handed it to her.

"You smoke first," he said.

She took it in her hands and putting it to her mouth pretended to draw in

BAH AND BILLY SMOKE THE PIPE OF PEACE

the smoke. She handed it to Billy, but he proceeded to bite out a piece, much to the astonishment of his playmate, who stared at him in wonderment.

"You do that, too, Bah, it's good," Billy mumbled with his mouth full.

Bah shrank back. "No, me no eat pipe, me smoke!"

Billy couldn't help laughing.

"Oh, but this isn't a real pipe—it's chocolate!"

Still Bah was reluctant to try.

"Well," said Billy, digging into his pocket for the rest of the candy. "Here's another, the same—only it's not in the shape of a pipe. Try it."

Bah took the candy and looked at it.

"Fish!" she gasped and dropped it.

"Well, what's the matter with that?" asked Billy, greatly disturbed by her evident horror.

"Bah no eat fish. No Navajo eat fish!" "Tell me why," said Billy, now amused and interested.

Bah did not answer, but pointed over to her mother. She hung her head shyly. Billy didn't like to press her, so, dragging his blanket, and with his crown over one ear, he stumbled over to the loom and stood before Mrs. Fighting Bull with the query: "Why don't Navajos like fish?"

Mrs. Fighting Bull did not smile, for once, and replied: "Not because no like! No eat because ancestors once turned into fish. If Navajo eat fish, he eat ancestor!"

Satisfied with this explanation, Billy thanked her and trotted back to his friend. "I understand now, Bah," he said. "But you see this isn't a real fish, it's candy! You try."

He held it up to her, but he could see how she shrank from the thought of eating anything that was even the shape of fish. So he picked out a bird and gave it to her. After she had sampled the chocolate she was delighted to finish the whole piece, and when that was eaten, she said: "Now me smoke pipe of peace."

"Yes," said Billy, "and this time you'll eat a piece of the pipe, won't you?"

He laughed loudly at his own joke, but Bah was too absorbed in her new found game. When Billy reached for the pipe, expecting to receive it for his turn, he saw that the little girl had put the whole pipe into her mouth and was munching the chocolate, her cheeks puffed out and a twinkle in her eye! Billy stared in surprise.

"Why, Bah, you bad girl. You ate up all the pipe!"

But they soon found another game to replace the "Peace Pipe" and played together happily until it was time for Billy to go home.

Before leaving he remembered that he had not thanked the Indian woman for telling him so much of interest. He ran back to where she was sitting, and, drawing from his pocket the chocolate candies, he offered them to her, saying: "Thanks so much for your nice story. Won't you have some candy?"

She took some and smiled at him. Then she said: "Write nice story about Indians. All white men no think Indians good."

Billy was puzzled for a moment to know what she meant. Then it dawned upon him that the Indians were often spoken of as cruel and savage. Well, he'd "tell the world" in his story that this family was kind and civilized. He said: "Oh, yes, I'll say everything I think about you, and that will be good!"

Then, suddenly bethinking himself of a word he'd once heard, he asked: "Isn't an Indian woman called a 'Squaw'?"

Bah's mother shook her head and a

THE "SQUAWKER"

slight frown—the first Billy had seen—appeared between her eyes.

"No. Indian woman no like to be called Squaw! Not very nice! In reservation she fight when man call that!"

"Well, I'll remember and never use

the word 'Squaw' again," promised Billy.

Just then an Indian mother appeared in the doorway of her hogan. The papoose upon her back was crying loudly, and Billy looked roguishly at Mrs. Fighting Bull and asked: "Is the baby called a 'Squawker'?"

CHAPTER VIII

WHO WINS THE RADIO?

For many days Billy worked diligently at his composition. He took care to do his writing away from home, as he cherished the thought of surprising Mother and Father.

Then, too, he had conceived another idea. It happened to pop into his head one evening when he was returning from Bah's home. It was such a good idea that he wondered he hadn't thought of it before.

And so, as I have said, he worked, and no one but Peanuts knew what he was doing, and Peanuts was sworn to se-

FOR DAYS BILLY WORKED ON HIS STORY

crecy. As he would prepare to leave his secluded spot out on the prairie where he did his writing, Billy would say to Peanuts: "Now, we'll never say a word! We'll keep this to ourselves, wont we?"

And Peanuts was most agreeable. Why not? The days had been pleasure since his master had decided to allow him to graze all day long instead of asking him to gallop over the plains. Yes, indeed, the plan suited Peanuts down to the ground (where, by the way, he constantly kept his nose.)

Billy's nose was buried in his writing and he chewed the pencil as steadily as Peanuts chewed the dry nourishment he found. But at last the task was over, the manuscript sent in to the magazine, and Billy was again paying his respects to the Fighting Bull family. Peanuts was the only regretful one when the story was finished, and sent away. Billy sighed a sigh of relief and the first day that he put in an appearance at the hogan, Bah squealed with joy to see him returning.

Many happy days ensued, in which the Indian girl showed the boy new games and ways of playing which she, little lonely one, had devised by herself.

Each evening Billy would come home with the same question on his lips: "Has my magazine arrived?"

But New York is a long way from Arizona, and it was many weeks before the magazine, in which the winning story was to appear, at last came.

It was one evening after Billy had had a particularly exciting day chas-

ing buffaloes (in the form of tame
sheep) with Bah, that he came home to
find his magazine awaiting him. It had
not been opened and was lying on his
little desk. It was addressed to him—
and inside it was—maybe—his story!
He longed to find out, but he couldn't
move his fingers to open the wrapper.

He suddenly grew hot all over and
realized then how he longed to see
that story inside those covers. If he
had been an Indian instead of a white
boy he would have made a prayer
stick and prayed via the eagle feather
to the Great Father.

The next morning Father and Mother found Billy curled up in a big chair
in the living room poring over his

magazine. They could not see his face.

Father took up his paper, but before starting to read he remarked: "Who's the lucky winner of the radio, Son?"

Billy did not answer, but arose from his chair and brought the magazine over to Father. Father glanced at the page with a wicked smile, and re-marked: "Needless to say, it wasn't a chap named William!"

Billy, his head drooping, left the room, and Mother felt sorry for him. So did Father. In fact I think Father was sorry for what he had said, as he got up and called him back.

It was then that Billy told Father what he had done—all about it from the first day that the idea had occurred to him until the moment when he had, with trembling fingers, opened the magazine and found . . . . .

"You're a good boy, Bill," said Father, "and I've been wronging you."

Mother was about to make a fuss over him, so, allowing her only time enough for one kiss, he grabbed his hat. Then with the parting words, "I'm going to see the Fighting Bulls—goodbye," he made a dash for the door.

"Some day maybe you'll take me, Bill," called Father after him, "I'd like to meet the Fighting Bulls, and their calf. She must be a smart little kid!"

Then the parents looked at each other and Mother's eyes were just a little bit dewy. She smiled and shook her finger at Father: "I know another Fighting Bull," she said.

"Yes, dear," said Father humbly, "and he has a splendid and plucky little calf!"

At the hogan there was much excitement. As Peanuts came galloping down the village "street" his rider saw a most unusual sight.

Chief Fighting Bull, his wife and small daughter were all grouped about an object which seemed to be attracting them. So much did it attract them that they were talking in Navajo faster and louder than Billy had ever heard them talk.

The boy jumped down from his pony and walked up to the family circle.

"IS IT FOR ME?"

He saw that the object of their interest was a large wooden express box, and written across it were the words:

"Bah, The Little Indian Weaver,
    Daughter of Chief Fighting Bull,
        Navajo Reservation, near Tuba, Arizona."

"This came today," said the Chief to Billy, and Bah held up an envelope which she clutched in her hand.

"And see—letter to Bah."

Billy asked: "Why don't you open it?"

"Yes, will do," replied the girl. At the same time as Bah and Billy were opening the letter, the Chief, aided by his wife, was opening the large box.

"You read letter for me, please," smiled Bah.

Billy took the letter—but just then the box was opened and inside it the astonished family beheld a radio!

"What this?" asked Fighting Bull.

Said Billy wisely: "It's a radio—you know, you can listen to music and

"WITHOUT YOU I COULDN'T HAVE WRITTEN IT."

everything. It's lots of fun. Come on, we'll fix it up!"

With Billy's instructions the Chief set up the radio. It was a portable set and as soon as they attached the aerial and Billy turned the dials the sound of fine music began to float on the air.

"Alive!" shrieked Bah, turned on her heels, and fled!

Billy, still holding the unopened letter, ran after her. He found her hidden in a thicket and brought her back to her parents, who stood transfixed before the radio, which was still sending forth music.

"Don't be afraid, Bah," said Billy. "It's not this box making the noise. The music comes through the air from a big city!"

The Chief and his wife were almost as impressed as Bah, but they did not show their feelings. They could only stand and stare while Billy, holding on to Bah with one hand for fear that she would run away again, read the following letter:

"Dear Little Bah:

Your story 'The Little Indian Weaver,' written by yourself about yourself, has won the Composition Contest. The prize, a radio, we are sending you today. It was a great pleasure to receive such a charming little story from a real Indian girl. The white children who read it will, we are sure, enjoy it, and learn a great deal from you. Thank you, and we hope you will like the radio!

The Children's Magazine."

"But—but," said Bah, "I not write story!"

Billy put his arm around her shoulders and smiling down at her said: "No, but I sent it in your name because if it hadn't been for you and your mother and father I never could have written it!"

"I PUT INDIAN FLAG ON MY SINGING BOX."

As the strains of music floated through the air, attracting the sheep from the prairie, two dreamy children sat beside the radio, which was perched on the top of a packing box, and listened eagerly.

THE WHITE CHILD LOVES HIS INDIAN FRIENDS

Bah had outgrown her fear of the "Singing Box" as she called the radio, and each day she and Billy would enjoy songs and music from the city—strange sounds, some of them, to the little Indian girl.

But to Billy it had become a greater joy than he ever had anticipated to watch her rapture with the new toy.

One day he found a stick with feathers stuck on top of the radio, and he asked her what it meant.

"Bah put flag on Singing Box. That is Indian flag!"

Billy never ceased learning about the Indians, their customs and their interesting ways.

Perhaps the Fighting Bulls also were learning. They learned what many Indians do not know—that the white child loves his brother—the first American.